E $7.96
Jo   Johnson, Audean
        A to Z look and
       see

DATE DUE

MR 7 '91	JUL 21 '94	NO 15 '06	AP 1 2 '17
AP 19 '91	MAR 03 '95	MR 02 '07	DY 05 '10
MY 16 '91	AUG 09 '95	DE 17 '08	
JE 24 '91	NOV 2 '98	DE 26 '08	
JE 27 '90	MAR 21 '96		
JY 9 '91	JL 25 '96	MY 04	JE 1 9 '2
AG 14 '91	AG 16 '00	JE 0 9 '0	
JY 13 '06	MY 03 02	JE 0 9 '09	JE 1 3 R
AG 13 '9	AP 24 '02	NO	
FE 15 '9	NO 15 '0	NE 7 5	MY 0 5 '1
FEB 16 '94	FE 24 '06	MA 1 3 '1	MR 1 6 '20
	OC 02 '0		

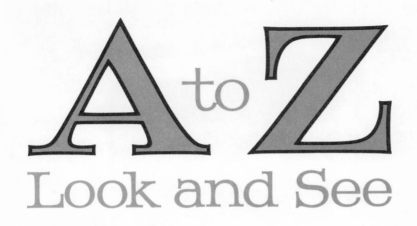

A to Z
Look and See

A Random House PICTUREBACK®

A to Z
Look and See

by AUDEAN JOHNSON

Random House  New York

A is for apple.

B is for butterfly.

C is for cat.

D is for doll.

E is for elephant.

F is for flower.

G is for goose.

H is for house.

I is for ice cream.

J is for jellybeans.

K is for kite.

L is for lamb.

M is for moon.

N is for nest.

O is for ostrich.

P is for paint.

Q is for quilt.

R is for rooster.

S is for scarecrow.

T is for truck.

U is for umbrella.

V is for vegetables.

W is for whistle.

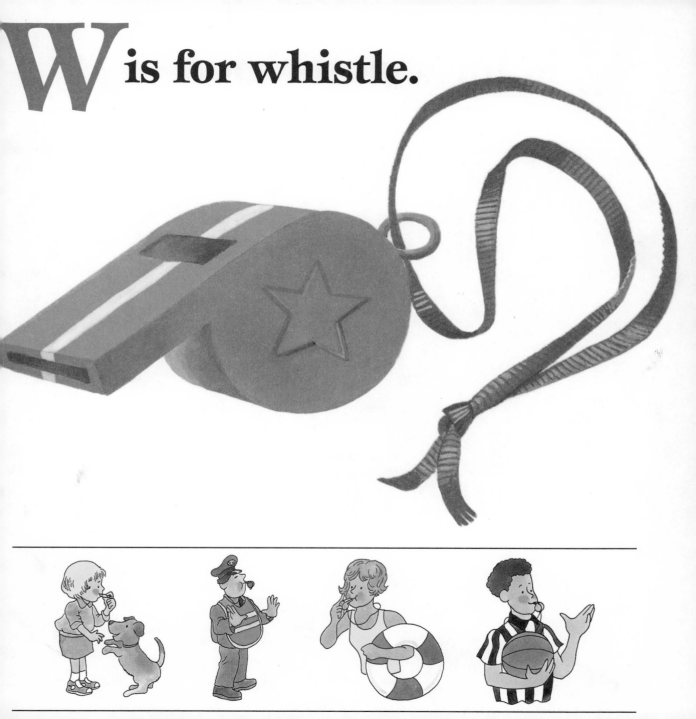

X is for xylophone.

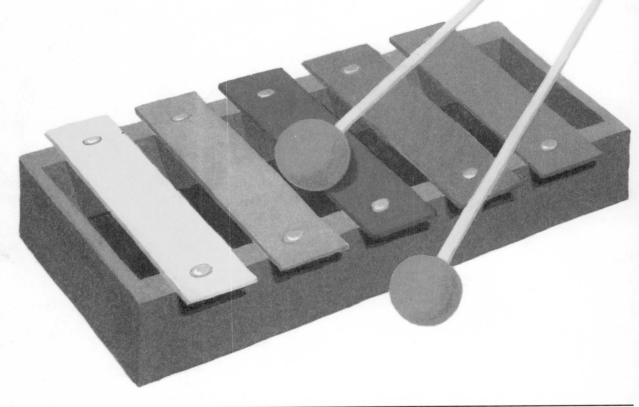

Y is for yarn.

Z is for zebra.

A to Z

Look and See!

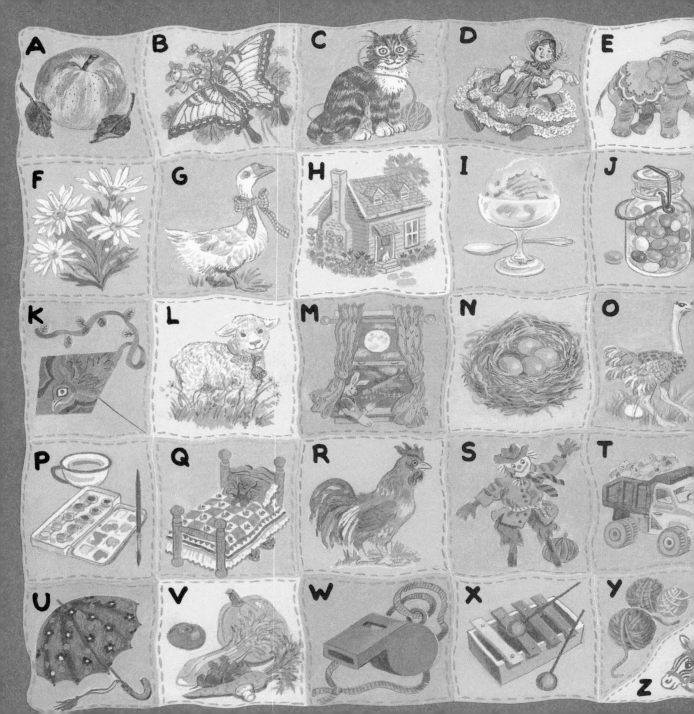